# THE CLONE WARS™

# BATTLE AT TETH

**Adapted by Kirsten Mayer**

**Based on the movie *Star Wars: The Clone Wars***

**Grosset & Dunlap · LucasBooks**

GROSSET & DUNLAP

Published by the Penguin Group

Penguin Group (USA) Inc., 375 Hudson Street, New York, New York 10014, USA

Penguin Group (Canada), 90 Eglinton Avenue East, Suite 700, Toronto, Ontario M4P 2Y3, Canada

(a division of Pearson Penguin Canada Inc.)

Penguin Books Ltd., 80 Strand, London WC2R 0RL, England

Penguin Group Ireland, 25 St. Stephen's Green, Dublin 2, Ireland

(a division of Penguin Books Ltd.)

Penguin Group (Australia), 250 Camberwell Road, Camberwell, Victoria 3124, Australia

(a division of Pearson Australia Group Pty. Ltd.)

Penguin Books India Pvt. Ltd., 11 Community Centre, Panchsheel Park, New Delhi—110 017, India

Penguin Group (NZ), 67 Apollo Drive, Rosedale, North Shore 0632, New Zealand

(a division of Pearson New Zealand Ltd.)

Penguin Books (South Africa) (Pty.) Ltd., 24 Sturdee Avenue,

Rosebank, Johannesburg 2196, South Africa

Penguin Books Ltd., Registered Offices:

80 Strand, London WC2R 0RL, England

*Library of Congress Cataloging-in-Publication Data is available.*

ISBN: 978-0-448-44993-7                                10 9 8

The galaxy is at war! The Jedi Knights and their trusty clone troopers fight for the Republic, protecting planets from large armies of battle droids. On the planet Teth, General Anakin Skywalker and clone Captain Rex lead a group of clone troopers on a rescue mission. A baby Hutt has been kidnapped. Can Rex hold off the droids until reinforcements arrive?

Clone Captain Rex went everywhere with Jedi General Anakin Skywalker. Rex was proud that the Jedi trusted him. Today, he would have many chances to prove his loyalty.

He stood near Skywalker on the gunship. As they came down toward the planet, the enemy battle droids on the surface of the planet opened fire.

"Close the blast shields!" Skywalker ordered the pilot.

"Get us in under those guns!"

Rex got his troops ready to land and told them to prepare their blasters. "Stand by!" he said.
The pilot managed to land the ship. The door opened into a steamy jungle.

"Green light! Go! Go! Go!" ordered Rex as all the troops rushed into the trees. Nearby, a castle loomed over the tangled vines at the top of a steep rock cliff.

Rex was right behind Skywalker as he charged for the castle. But as they scrambled up the rock wall, spider droids swarmed down around them.

The Jedi general quickly blasted through them.
"Follow General Skywalker!" Rex ordered the troopers as
he climbed up in Skywalker's wake.

At the top of the wall, the small army was met with fire from more droids. As Skywalker cut them down with his lightsaber, the clone troopers dispatched the rest of the spider droids.

Captain Rex finally reported, "All clear, General."
"Nice work, Rex. Have some men look after the wounded,"
said Skywalker.

Now it was time to rescue the Huttlet. The iron door creaked open to reveal a long dark tunnel.

"I don't like this place," said Rex. "It gives me the creeps."

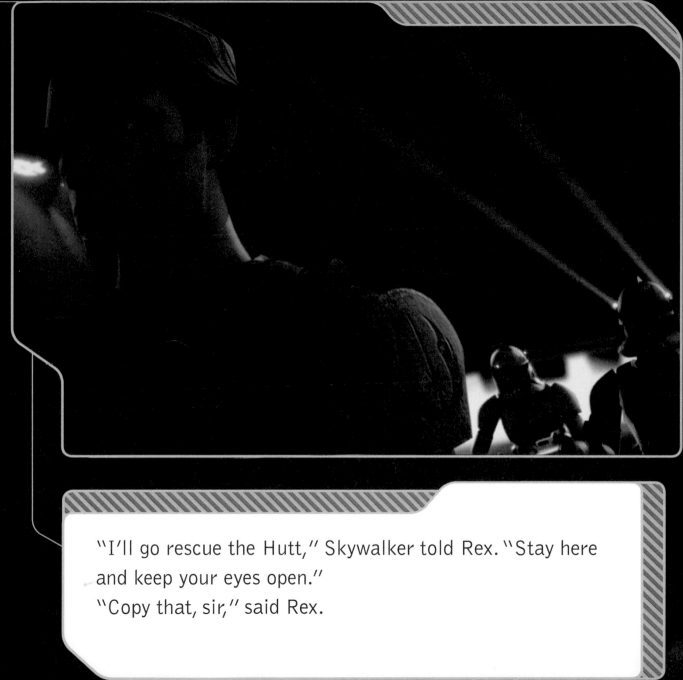

"I'll go rescue the Hutt," Skywalker told Rex. "Stay here and keep your eyes open."

"Copy that, sir," said Rex.

Out in the castle courtyard, Rex waited for Skywalker to return. There was no sign of droids and it seemed too quiet. Suddenly, Skywalker burst out of the castle carrying the baby Hutt.

Just then, Rex looked up to see enemy fighter ships coming in through the clouds.

"Defensive positions!" yelled Rex, and the troopers scrambled into place.

The ships blasted the area and droids swarmed into the courtyard. The clone troopers were driven back up into the castle.

"Fall back! Fall back!" ordered Skywalker. Rex got everyone inside the castle.

Protecting his men, Skywalker continued slashing droids with his lightsaber until he finally rolled underneath the closing castle door.

Inside the castle, Skywalker said, "Hold them here as long as you can."

Rex nodded. "Will do, sir."

He watched Skywalker head deeper into the castle with the baby Hutt. He knew the Jedi had a plan to get the Hutt out.

Rex turned to his troops. "You heard the general. Get
ready to turn those clankers into scrap metal."
They lined the walls, and locked and loaded for the
oncoming droids.

The door began to inch open. "They've cut the lock!"
yelled a trooper. Droids poured in, firing everywhere. The
clones returned fire.

"Hold the line!" yelled Rex. "Watch your left!"
Suddenly, there was a huge explosion!

When the dust cleared, the dark assassin named Asajj Ventress entered the castle to speak with the droid commander. Clone Captain Rex was stunned and lying on the ground, but he could hear everything she said. "Seal the entrance. Let nothing escape this castle," she told the droid.

Rex reached for his blaster and before Ventress could react, he blasted the droid. His second shot was aimed at her, but she quickly ignited her lightsaber and blocked it.

Enraged, Ventress used the Force to toss Rex's blaster away and lift him off the ground.

"Where is Skywalker?" she demanded.

"I don't talk to scum," said the loyal Rex. He would never betray his general.

Ventress was furious. She knocked Rex out and left him in a heap.

When he woke up, Rex found himself under droid guard with the other troopers. His wrist communication unit was crackling.

"Do you copy? This is Skywalker, over. Rex?"

The droid guards heard the noise and came closer to investigate. Rex held his arm up and waited for them to get really close. One of the droids leaned in . . . and Rex punched it.

"Let me show you how it works, clanker!"

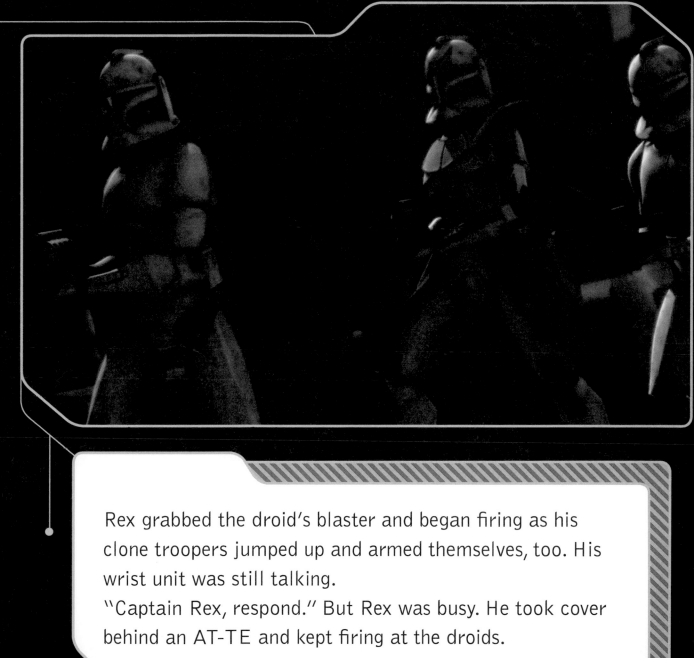

Rex grabbed the droid's blaster and began firing as his clone troopers jumped up and armed themselves, too. His wrist unit was still talking.

"Captain Rex, respond." But Rex was busy. He took cover behind an AT-TE and kept firing at the droids.

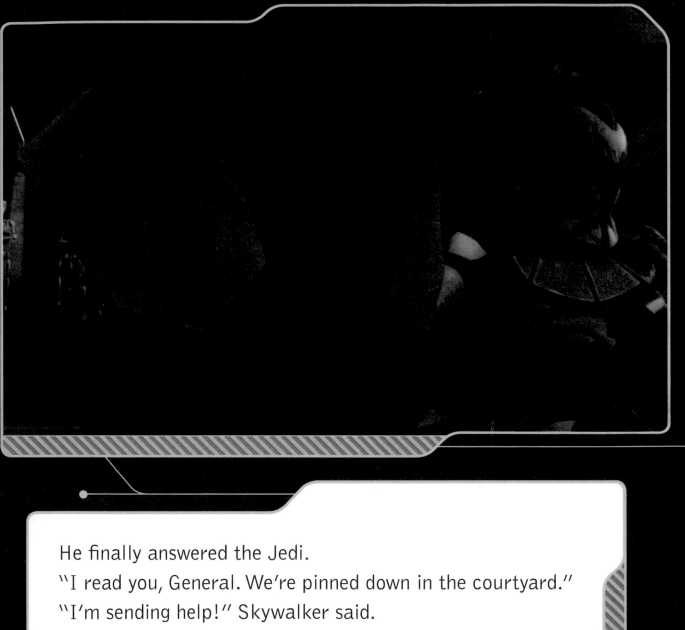

He finally answered the Jedi.

"I read you, General. We're pinned down in the courtyard."

"I'm sending help!" Skywalker said.

The troopers continued to blast at droids, but more just kept coming. Things were starting to look grim for Rex. One of his troopers looked to the skies. "We can't hold out much longer, sir! Where's General Skywalker?"

"He'll be here!" barked Rex. He knew his general wouldn't abandon them.

"This is it!" he yelled to rally his troops. "Scrap 'em!"
But the clones were completely surrounded.
"Surrender!" yelled the droid commander.
"We've got you outnumbered!" Rex yelled back.

The droid was confused. It started counting the small number of clone troopers. "One, two, three . . ." *BLAM!* The droid exploded as a Jedi interceptor screamed through the air over the castle.

Backup had finally arrived!

Clone Captain Rex grabbed a grenade and dove under a spider droid. With an explosion, the remains of the droid collapsed to the ground. Rex and his troops were successful in holding off the enemy. And because of their courage and loyalty, Anakin Skywalker was able to complete his mission, and the Jedi were one step closer to defeating the Sith.